Everyone is scared of something.

Living with fear can make even the bravest person feel small.

Emily Gravett's

Big Book of Fears

is *the* essential book to help you overcome your phobias.

It has been put together by an expert in worrying,
who draws on a lifetime's experience of managing
her fears through the medium of doodle.

You too can overcome your fears through the use of art!

Each page in this book provides a large blank space
for you to record and face your fear using a combination of:

Drawing

Writing

Collage.

REMEMBER!

A FEAR FACED IS A FEAR DEFEATED.

SIMON & SCHUSTER BOOKS FOR YOUNG READERS
An imprint of Simon & Schuster Children's Publishing Division
1230 Avenue of the Americas, New York, New York 10020

First published in Great Britain in 2007 by Macmillan Children's Books, London
First U.S. edition 2008

SIMON & SCHUSTER BOOKS FOR YOUNG READERS
is a trademark of Simon & Schuster, Inc.

The text for this book is set in New Baskerville and hand lettering.
The illustrations are rendered in oil-based pencil and watercolor on Saunders Waterford hot-pressed paper and found objects.
Nibbled paper edges were provided by Emily's daughter's pet rats, Button and Mr. Moo.
Manufactured in China

2 4 6 8 10 9 7 5 3

CIP data for this book is available from the Library of Congress.

ISBN-13: 978-1-4169-5930-4
ISBN-10: 1-4169-5930-0

Entomophobia
(*Fear of insects*)

Use the space below to record your fears.

Use the space below to record your fears.

I worry about what's under the bed.

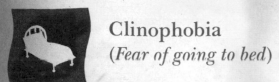

Clinophobia
(*Fear of going to bed*)

Use the space below to record your fears.

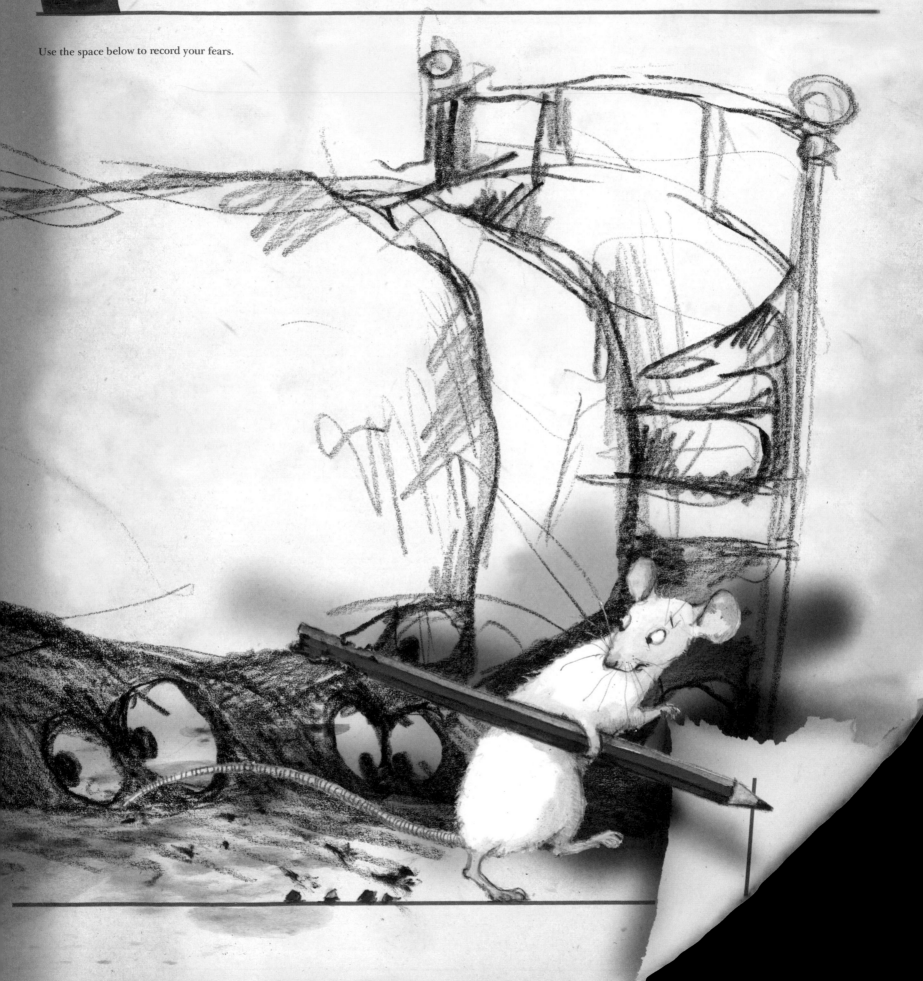

Aichmophobia
(Fear of knives)

Use the space below to record your fears.

I get edgy near sharp knives.

Get Well Soon

THE AMAZING FLYING MOUSECROBATS

CIRCUS

CANCELLED

DID YOU EVER SEE SUCH A THING IN YOUR LIFE?

THE AMAZING MOUSECROBAT TRIO ARE COMPLETELY BLIND!
SEE HOW THEY PERFORM USING ONLY THEIR TAILS AND SENSE OF SMELL
TO GUIDE THEM!

THREE BLIND MICE

The Farmer's Friend

ne Farmer's Frienc

News, views, and moos from down on th

Mouse numb

Tail End for Deep Cut Farm's Mouse Problem

by M. Ferguson

Deep Cut Farm of Lower Wallop is enjoying its first mouse-free evening for weeks after a recent assault by a trio of cheese-mad rodents made life intolerable on the once peaceful dairy farm.

Matters came to a head last Saturday when Mrs. Sabatier, wife of Farmer Sabatier (Best Big Cheese Award Winner 2005), decided that enough was enough.

"The blinking mice had been driving me mad! They were running after me while I was working. I think they could smell the cheese!" she fumed. "I just lost it, I was blind mad! I picked up the nearest thing to hand, which was my carving knife, and before I knew what I had done, there were three tails in my hand, and three mice running as fast as their legs could carry them out of the door."

Well, one thing's for certain, that's the last time

Mrs. Sabatier, triumpha

A̲MAZIN̲

CA

that, due to

performanc

per

Ablutophobia
(Fear of bathing)

Use the space below to record your fears.

Hydrophobia
(Fear of water)

Use the space below to record your fears.

or

flushed down

the toilet.

Use the space below t

BATHROOMS

Toilets to Go!

Super Deluxe Luxury 'Derrière' Toilet

SUPER SAVER

The Super Deluxe Luxury 'Derrière' range of sanitary ware is the best that money can buy. The satin smooth porcelain ensures ease of cleaning for even the most stubborn marks and stains. The ergonomically engineered seat incorporates Warm Rear® technology for a comfortable and enjoyable experience.

ME (TINY)

SEAT TOO HIGH

Serial No.	Type
123.44	Soft cream / Extra high seat
123.45	White / White / Chrome High
123.46	Extra powerful flush (for large famil)
123.47	Economy flush (not for heavy loads)
123.48	High-level (Extra whoosh!)
123.49	Push flush
123.50	Close-coupled pan

Could I build this in time?

✓ NEW

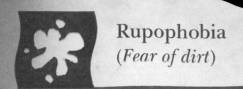

Rupophobia
(*Fear of dirt*)

Use the space below to record your fears.

I worry about
having accidents.

Ligyrophobia
(Fear of loud noises)

I'M ALARMED BY

HICKORY

Hickory Dicko...
The mou...
The clock str...
The m...
Hick...

Chronomentrophobia
(*Fear of clocks*)

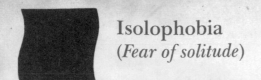

Isolophobia
(*Fear of solitude*)

Use the space below to record your fears.

I don't like being alone, or in the dark.

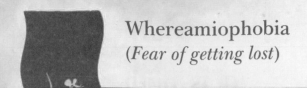

Whereamiophobia
(*Fear of getting lost*)

Use the space below to record your fears.

I'm scared of getting lost....

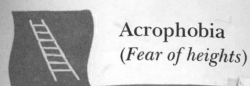

Acrophobia
(*Fear of heights*)

Use the space below to record your fears.

Ornithophobia
(*Fear of birds*)

Use the space below to record your fears.

Birds make me feel twitchy.

Phagophobia
(*Fear of being eaten*)

Use the space below to record your fears.

woof!

Cynophobia
(*Fear of dogs*)

Use the space belo............rd your fears.

I get nervous near dogs.

Ailuroph

(Fear of c

Use the space below to record your

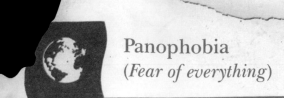

Panophobia
(Fear of everything)

Use the space below to record your fears.

I'm afraid of nearly EVERYTHING I see.

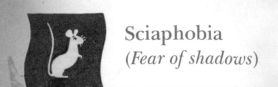

Sciaphobia
(Fear of shadows)

Use the space below to record your fears.

But even though I'm very small...

Use the space below to record your fears.

she's afraid of

ME!

Bibliophobia
(Fear of books)

Use the space below to record your fears.